Produced by
TWIN BOOKS
Kimbolton House
117a Fulham Road
London SW3 6RL

Directed by CND – Muriel Nathan-Deiller
Illustrated by Van Gool-Lefèvre-Loiseaux

ISBN: 1 85469 782 X

Printed in China

The Little Mermaid

Van Gool

TWIN BOOKS

Many years ago there was a beautiful palace at the very bottom of the sea. This was the home of six beautiful mermaid sisters. They lived with their parents, the King and Queen of the sea. The mermaids had tails instead of legs and every day they swam in the palace gardens, playing among the brightly coloured plants and fish.

The mermaids were very curious, and loved to ask their parents about the world around them. One evening the eldest mermaid asked her parents, "Tell us about the world above the sea." The other mermaids crowded around the King and Queen. "It is a beautiful country," said the Queen. "The people there have two legs instead of a tail!" The mermaids laughed at the thought. "Can we go and visit?" they begged, but their father replied, "Not until your fifteenth birthday."

The years passed. As each mermaid had her fifteenth birthday she swam to the surface to look at the world above the waves. The Little Mermaid listened longingly as each of her sisters described the beautiful things she had seen. Finally it was the Little Mermaid's turn.

"Take care," said her mother. "Keep away from humans and don't let anyone see you." "You'll have a wonderful time!" cried her sisters. "Tell us everything when you get back!" Full of excitement the Little Mermaid swam towards the surface. "I can hardly believe that I am going to see all the wonderful things my sisters have spoken of," she thought to herself.

When she reached the surface, the Little Mermaid peeked above the waves. In delight she gazed at a ship sailing past, its white sails billowing in the breeze. The decks were hung with brightly coloured lanterns and she could hear music and singing coming from on board. Curious, she swam a little closer.

A wave lifted her up so she could see on to the deck. It was full of people dancing, laughing and talking. “It’s a party!” murmured the Little Mermaid. “I wonder what it is for?” Just then a young man appeared on the deck. The music stopped and everyone began to cheer.

"Happy birthday to our Prince!" cheered the sailors. The young Prince smiled. "Thank you, my friends!" he cried. "Now let the party continue!" And he stepped down to join the men on the deck.

The Little Mermaid thought the young Prince was very handsome. But she was so busy watching the party that she did not see the storm clouds approaching. The wind whipped the sails to tatters, and huge waves tossed the ship from side to side. The sailors tried to save their ship, but it was too late. The great mast splintered and water crashed on to the deck.

In horror the Little Mermaid saw a great wave sweep the young Prince into the sea. He had been knocked unconscious, and she swam to save him. Using all her strength the Little Mermaid held on to the Prince's jacket, and pulled him to shore. Gently she laid him on the sand. She smoothed back his hair, and sang to him softly to try to awaken him.

Suddenly she heard voices. Three young girls were walking down the beach from the castle. At once the Little Mermaid dived back into the sea, for she did not dare to let a human see her.

When she returned to the palace under the sea, her family were eager to hear what she had seen. But she shook her head sadly, and told them nothing. She no longer played with her sisters, or joined in when they begged their parents for stories. Instead she found a quiet corner, far from the palace, and sat by herself. A piece of the Prince's jacket had torn when she rescued him, and she would sit and hold it, dreaming of seeing him once more.

Finally she plucked up courage to go and visit the sea witch, who lived at the bottom of a deep cave. The witch was very powerful, and the Little Mermaid felt afraid. "Please help me," she begged. "I must see my Prince again!" "I will give you legs so you can join your Prince," said the sea witch. "But you must give me something in return. You must give me your beautiful voice."

Without hesitating the Little Mermaid agreed to the witch's bargain. At once she felt a tingling in her throat, but when she went to speak, no sound came out. Her voice was gone! Mutely she watched as the witch mixed up a magic potion and poured it into a glass bottle. "Take this," said the witch. "Swim to the beach where you left the Prince and drink it. It will change your tail into legs to walk with."

The Little Mermaid swam to the beach and sat on the sand. Nervously she opened the bottle. "Will it hurt?" she wondered. She hesitated for a moment, then lifted the bottle to her lips and drank the potion. Almost at once she felt giddy, and the world began to swim around her.

Her tail felt as if it were burning but she could not make a sound. The Little Mermaid fainted on the sand.

When the Little Mermaid awoke, a young man was standing by her. It was the Prince! "I was worried about you," he said. "Are you feeling better?" The Little Mermaid could only nod.

"Come with me," said the Prince, handing her his cloak. "I will take you to my father's castle." The Little Mermaid looked down, and almost gasped in delight. Instead of a tail she had a lovely pair of legs! At first it was painful to walk, and the Prince had to help her up the beach.

That evening there was a great ball at the palace. The Prince danced with the Little Mermaid, then left her to go and talk with another young lady. She was one of the girls who had walked down to the beach after she had saved the Prince. To her horror she learned that the Prince thought this girl had saved him – and he was going to marry her! "If only I could tell him the truth!" thought the Little Mermaid in despair.

The next day the Little Mermaid ran down to the beach. She knew her sisters often came there to play in the sun. As soon as they saw her, they knew something was wrong. "What is it, little sister," they asked, but she could not tell them. Finally the eldest said, "Whatever it is, the sea witch will know. We will go and ask her for help."

The four sisters swam down to the witch's cave. "I know what is wrong with your little sister, girls," said the witch. "And I will help her once more. I have seen how much she loves her Prince, and she deserves to be happy. Here, take this potion to her, and tell her it will bring her voice back." At once the mermaids swam back to their sister, and gave her the bottle.

They had been just in time, for the Prince's wedding was about to take place on the royal yacht. The Little Mermaid hurried on board, and sipped the potion. She felt her voice return, and began to sing. The Prince turned towards her, for he recognised the song she had sung to him on the beach. "It was you!" he exclaimed.

The Little Mermaid explained how she had saved him, and as she spoke the Prince fell in love with her. "You must never leave me again!" he exclaimed. The Little Mermaid handed him the magic potion. "Drink this," she whispered. "It will help you come with me to my kingdom under the sea."

"You came to my kingdom to find me," said the Prince, "I will gladly follow you under the sea." He drank the potion, then turned to the Little Mermaid and took her hand. Together they dived into the deep blue sea and swam far beneath the waves.

The King and Queen were delighted to see their youngest daughter again. Her sisters had told their parents about the Prince, and they greeted the young man warmly. "Welcome to our kingdom," declared the King, and when the Prince asked for the Little Mermaid's hand in marriage, he gladly agreed.

A great celebration was prepared, and everyone under the sea was invited to the wedding. The feasting, music and dancing went on for three days. When the party was over, the King gave the Prince and the Little Mermaid a beautiful golden carriage pulled by four seahorses. Everyone came out to wave goodbye to the happy couple as they set off on their honeymoon.

When they returned, the Prince and his mermaid bride lived happily in the royal palace with her parents. Many years later they became King and Queen themselves, and ruled well and wisely over their subjects. Even today people talk about their wonderful wedding party, and everyone agrees that there has never been such a happy couple as the Little Mermaid and her Prince.